To my family and Win

First Edition, September 2017
10 9 8 7 6 5 4 3 2 1
FAC-029191-17160
Printed in Malaysia

This book is set in 18-point Strima/Fontspring
Designed by Joann Hill
Illustrations created using watercolor, color pencil, ink, and Photoshop.

Library of Congress Cataloging-in-Publication Data
Names: Kang, A. N., author.
Title: Papillon goes to the vet / by A. N. Kang.
Description: First edition. • Los Angeles ; New York : Disney-Hyperion,
   [2017] • Series: Papillon ; 2 • Summary: When Papillon's hiccups cause him
   to stop floating, Miss Tilly rushes him to a clinic where, once he feels
   better, he makes new friends.
Identifiers: LCCN 2016034311 • ISBN 9781484728819 (hardcover) • ISBN
   1484728815 (hardcover)
Subjects: CYAC: Cats—Fiction. Sick—Fiction. Veterinary
   Hospitals—Fiction. Friendship—Fiction. Humorous stories.
Classification: LCC PZ7.1.K26 Pap 2017 • DDC [E]—dc23
LC record available at https://lccn.loc.gov/2016034311

Reinforced binding
Visit www.DisneyBooks.com

THE VERY FLUFFY KITTY

Papillon
Goes to the Vet

hic

BY A. N. KANG

𝒟isney • HYPERION

Los Angeles   New York

Papillon is a very fluffy cat.

He can float like a cloud in the sky.

He loves to play
with his friend.
They never tire of
playing kung fu air kicks
and yarn softball.

But catch is their
favorite game.

One day, something went terribly wrong.

Oh, poor Papillon!
He didn't feel well at all.
He had hiccups that
wouldn't stop.
But the worst thing was . . .

He could no longer float!

Miss Tilly rushed him to the kitty clinic to see the vet.

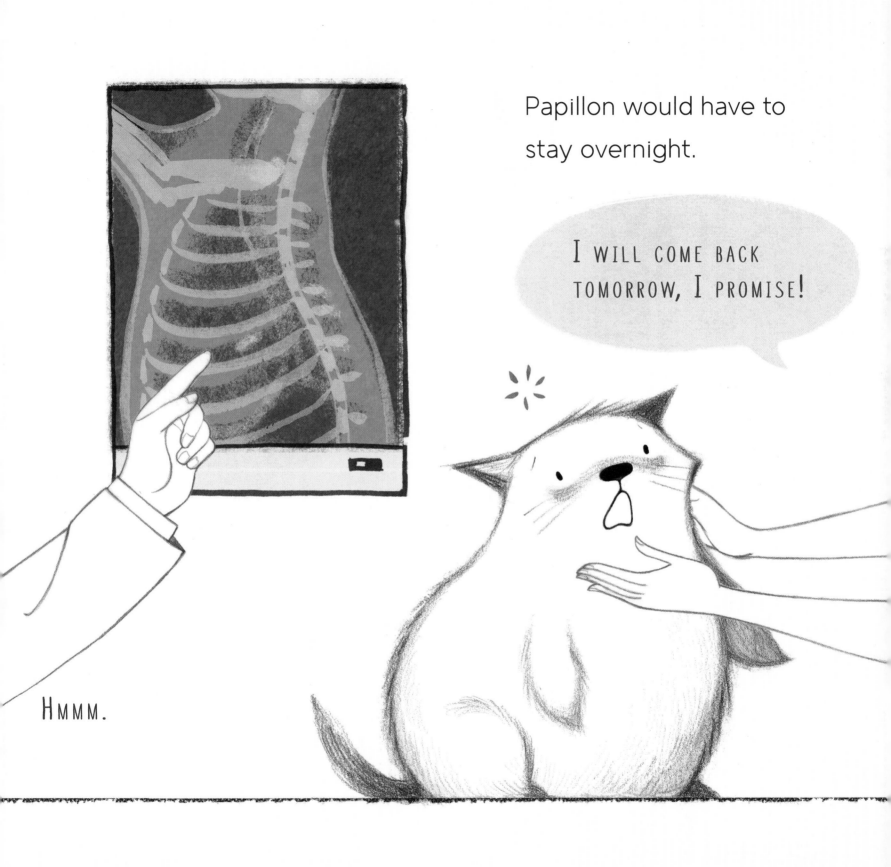

Papillon would have to stay overnight.

I WILL COME BACK TOMORROW, I PROMISE!

HMMM.

There were other
cats at the clinic,
who were beautiful

and very talented.

Papillon didn't feel either
beautiful or talented.
He felt all alone.
He just wanted to go home.

hic hic

hiccup

hic

hic hic

Crying made his hiccups worse! Then . . .

Papillon was so much better.
He felt like dancing!

So Papillon showed off
his dance moves,

and his beautiful singing voice. Everyone was very impressed.

That night, Papillon played
with many new friends.
He even showed them how
to play catch.

And the next day, the most amazing kitty, Papillon, came home.

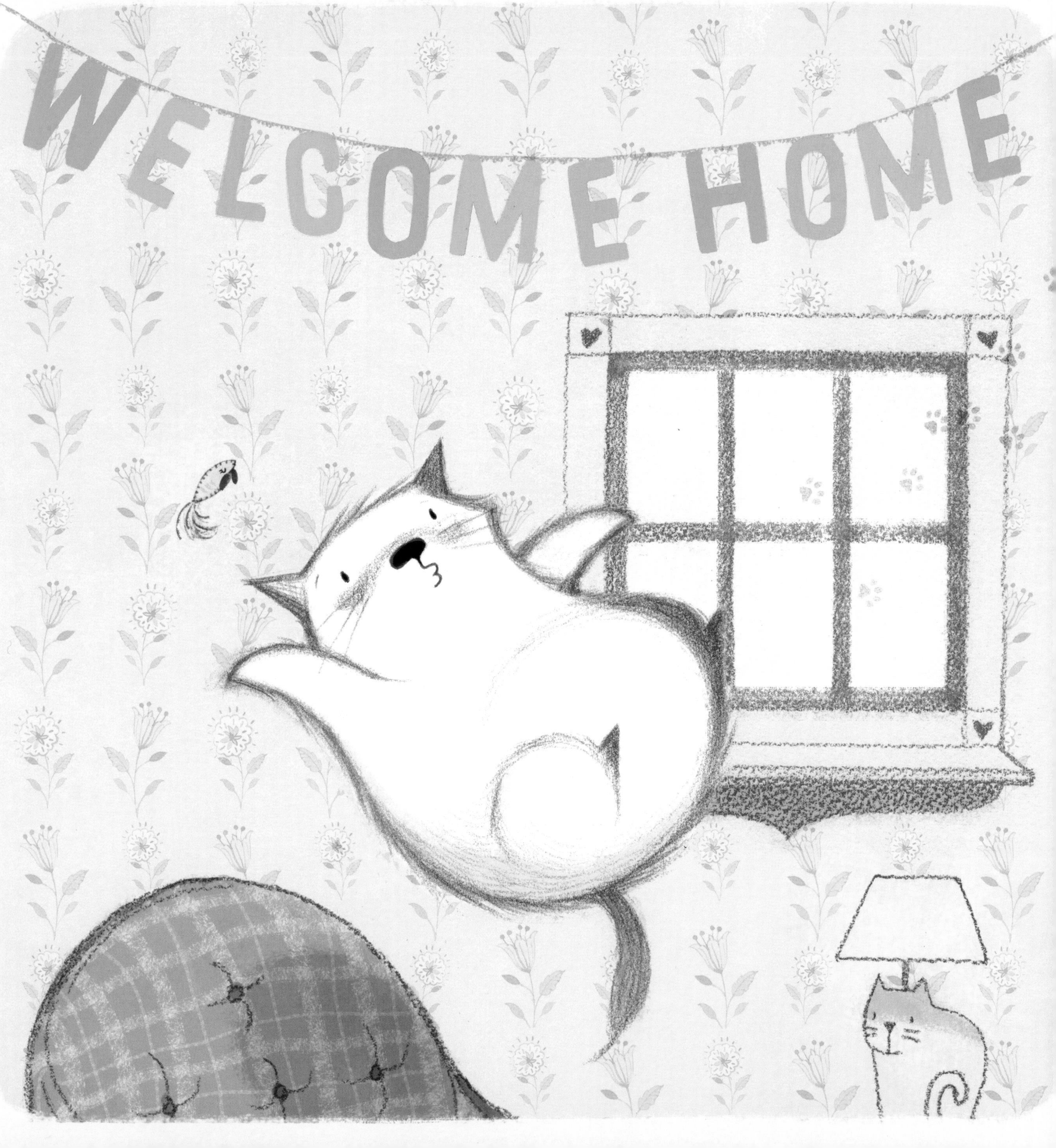
WELCOME HOME

PAPILLON

Papillon was happy to play
catch with his friend again,
but this time, Papillon kept
his mouth closed tight!